FLORENCE WARD'S

Victorian Birthday Book

FLORENCE WARD'S

Victorian Birthday Book

Webb & Bower

EXETER, ENGLAND

Published in Great Britain 1981 by
Webb & Bower (Publishers) Limited
33 Southernhay East, Exeter, Devon EX1 1NS

Designed by Malcolm Couch

British Library Cataloguing in Publication Data
Ward, Florence
  Florence Ward's Victorian birthday book.
  1. Anniversaries   2. Ward, Florence
  394.2   GT3930
  ISBN 0–906671–16–7

Phototypeset in Great Britain by Filmtype Services Limited, Scarborough

Printed and bound in Hong Kong by Mandarin Offset
International Limited

Birthday Book

Monday's bairn is fair of face,
Tuesday's bairn is full of grace,
Wednesday's bairn is a child of woe,
Thursday's bairn has far to go.
Friday's bairn is loving and giving,
Saturday's bairn works hard for his
                                    living.
The bairn that's born on the Sabbath
                                    day
Is bonny and healthy, wise and gay.

Names familiar and beloved
Cyphered here on mortal page,
Many a chord ye strike of memory,
Ranging wide from youth to age.
As we scan the trace of fingers
We have clasped in days of yore,
As we think of lights and shadows
Chequered round our path no more.

Florence Ward 1891

FLORENCE WARD
1864–1916

Florence was born on 5th May 1864 at 1 Claremont Place, Sheffield. Her father was Benjamin Burdekin, born in 1831, who in 1855 qualified as a solicitor and his firm still exists to this day. In 1858 he married Sarah Ann Rogers and their daughter Florence was the only girl in a family of five sons. Little is known of Florence's childhood, but the family continued to live in Sheffield, and her father became a respected member of the community. He was given the task in 1899 of drawing the attention of the Sheffield Corporation to the bad effects on the city of factory smoke, becoming honorary secretary of the Sheffield Smoke Abatement Association. (Sheffield today is considered one of the cleanest industrial cities in the north of England.)

As reported in a local newspaper, in

July 1888 at St Mark's Church, Sheffield, Florence, aged twenty-four, married David Ward, the son of a successful local businessman. David's father was an astute and progressive man who had set up a firm of edge-tool manufacturers. He was elected Lord Mayor of Sheffield in 1878, and did much to alleviate the poverty of the times. He was involved in charitable work such as the institution of a local fund to which he himself contributed generously, and in the distribution of free food to the needy. He was also involved in the building of St Mark's Church in which Florence and David were married. When he died in 1889 David was left to carry on the business with his brother Herbert.

After they were married Florence and David moved to The Beeches, Baslow, Derbyshire. They had two sons, David Leslie, born in November 1888 and Stanley, born in January 1894. David Leslie eventually took over the business from his father when he retired at the beginning of World War I.

It was during the early years of her marriage that Florence compiled and painted her Birthday Book, and it is remarkable that the technical excellence and freshness of the paintings were apparently achieved without formal training in art.

Tragically, when in her forties, Florence became ill and virtually crippled, so that she became confined to a wheelchair. She died on 20th September 1916, thirty years before her husband, and was buried in the family vault in Sheffield.

Write your name upon my page,
For – though we may sever,
Friendship is a heritage
That may last for ever.

Write it, and 'twill speak to you,
Write it, for a token
That our Friendship's tried and true,
And never will be broken.

'Tis by little links like these,
Lives are bound together.
Through the hours of toil and ease,
Glad and gloomy weather.

Birthday Book.

January

2.

A beautiful maid
Is a charming sight to see.

1.

Two is company, three is none.

January

3.

Win straying souls,
Cast none away.

Be strong!   be good!   be pure!

4.

Bliss and goodness on you.

He makes a July's day short as December.

January

5.

For a light heart lives long.

6.

Prosperity by thy page!

7.

I forgive and quite forget old faults.

He's honest, on mine honour.

January

9.

A kind heart he hath.

Is she not passing fair?

8.

In faith, he is a worthy gentleman,
Exceedingly well-read.

She is an earthly paragon.

January

10.

All happiness bechance to thee.

11.

He hath an excellent good name.

January

13.

*I'm never known to quail
At the fury of the gale.*

12.

*You were born under
a charitable star.*

January

15.

*In all things mindful not of herself,
but bearing the burdens of others.*

14.

*A town that boasts
    inhabitants like me,*

*Can have no lack
    of good society.*

16.

*Noble by birth, yet nobler
            by great deeds.
Flow, you heavenly blessings on her!*

January

17.

*alseness cannot come
from thee.*

My man's as true as steel.

18.

*I count myself in nothing
else so happy
As in a soul remembering
my good friends.*

19.

In maiden meditation fancy-free.

Many years of happy days befall thee.

January

21.

Men of few words are the best.

A constant woman.

20.

Friend to truth, of soul sincere,
In actions faithful, in honour clear.

January

22.

Fair, strong and tall!

Happy be thy life, O maid.

23.

Your object all sublime
You will achieve in time.

24.

She is just the sort of girl I like,
You know I do.

A good heart's worth gold.

January

25.

God bless thee.

26.

His hand is ready and willing.
How lady-like, how queen-like.

January

27.

The hand that made you fair hath made you good.

28.

Bid her have good heart.

January

29.

*You have deserved
High commendation, true applause
and love.*

30.

*I wish you all the joy that
you can wish.*

January

31.

A soul as full of worth,

    as void of pride.

Long may you live in fortune.

February

1.

Sacred and sweet was all I saw in her.

2.

He hath a stern look, but a gentle heart.

3.

Heaven give you many many happy days.

February

5.

Here is a true industrious friend.

4.

A learned spirit of human dealings.

February

6.

He is your friend for ever.

7.

Came of a gentle, kind and noble stoc

February

8.

O, he's the very soul of bounty.

10.

How far can I praise him?

9.

I am as tough as a bone,
With a will of my own.

February

11.

I am the very pink of courtesy.

12.

He's honest, on mine honour.

February

13.

He will keep that good name still.

Heaven bless thee.

14.

I have heard of the lady, and good words went with her name.

February

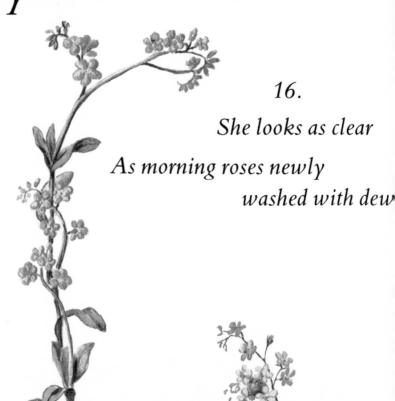

15.

A good heart's worth gold.

God bless thee, lady.

16.

She looks as clear

As morning roses newly

washed with dew

February

17.

God bless thee; and put meekness in thy mind,
Love, charity, obedience, and true duty.

18.

Her words do show her wit incomparable.

February

19.

Speak freely what you think.

20.

*Take him and use him well,
he's worthy of it.*

February

21.

know you have a gentle, noble temper,

A soul as even as a calm.

22.

Of many good I think him best.

Gentle art thou, and therefore to be won.

February

23.

For a light heart lives long.

24.

*Hearing you praised, I say, ''Tis so,
'tis true.' And to the most of praise
add something more.*

February

25.

She's a good creature.

26.

You have deserved
High commendation, true applause, and love.

February

27.

Take from my mouth the wish
of happy years.

28.

He that is thy friend indeed,
He will help thee in thy need.

February

29.

In thy face I see
The map of honour, truth and loyalty.

MARCH

Sweet March days
With skies of grey,
And winds which breathe
Of coming May.

New life, new love, new leafage,
For ever old and young,
In all the flowers that open,
In all the songs that are sung.

March

1.

How far can I praise him?

She is young, and of a modest nature.

2.

A rarer spirit never
Did steer humanity.

3.

A kind heart he hath.

Is she not passing fair?

March

5.

My gentle lady.

I wish you all the joy that you can wish.

For a light heart lives long.

4.

...ake from my mouth the wish
of happy years.

March

6.

You were born under a charitable star.

7.

Sir, as I have a soul,
she is an angel!

March

8.

To be merry best becomes you,
for, out of all question, you were
born in a merry hour.

9.

Fortune and Victory sit on
thy helm.

She is of so free, so kind, so apt,
so blessed a disposition.

10.

God bless thee, lady.
Few words to fair faith.

March

11.

A merrier man,
Within the limit of becoming mirt
I never spent an hour's talk witha

12.

Your name, fair gentlewoman?

March

13.

He is simply the rarest man
                i' the world.

15.

And having sworn truth,
                ever will be true.

Thy truth then be thy dower.

14.

'Tis death to me to be at enmity;
I hate it, and desire all good men's love.

March

16.

*To thee and thy company I bid
A hearty welcome.*

17.

*The gravity and stillness of
your youth
The world hath noted.*

18.

*The elements be kind to thee, and make
Thy spirits all of comfort.*

March

19.

O, he's the very soul of bounty.

20,

God be wi'you, with all my heart.

For I profess not talking; only this —
Let each man do his best.

21.

I have a man's mind, but a
woman's might.

March

22.

How far can I praise him?
Exceeding wise, fair-spoken,
　　　　and persuading.

23.

I would applaud thee to the very echo,
That should applaud again.

March

24.

What stature is she of?
Just as high as my heart.

25.

A man of good repute, carriage,
bearing and estimation.

26.

Thou art as wise as thou art beautiful.

March

27.

Flow, ye heavenly blessings on her!

To be a peacemaker shall
             become my age.

28.

Mine eyes

Were not in fault, for she was
             beautiful

March

29.

I know the gentleman
To be of worth and worthy estimation.

30.

O while you live tell truth
and shame the devil.

31.

Good fortune guide thee.

Oh to be in England
Now that April's there,
And whosoever wakes in England
Sees, some morning, unawares,
That the lowest boughs, and
                        the brush sheaf
Round the elm-tree hole are in tiny leaf.

April

1.

You bear a gentle mind, and
            heavenly blessings
Follow such creatures.

2.

By my prayers
For ever and for ever shall be you

3.

Thou hast mettle enough in thee to kill care.

April

4.

Seeks to aid

The orphan, the friendless one, the luckless or the poor.

5.

Thou hast the sweetest face I ever looked on.

April

6.

Sweets to the sweets.

7.

She's a good creature.

I'll note you in my book of memory

8.

Look what is best, that best I wish in thee.

April

9.

A double blessing is a double grace.

10.

He will keep that good name still.
Courage and comfort!
all shall yet go well.

11.

Busy after others good, for herself
The last to care.
Let our old acquaintance be renewed.

April

12.

I like your silence, it the more shows off
Your wonder.

13.

A cold and clear-cut face,
Perfectly beautiful.

April

14.

He hath a tear for pity, and a hand
Open as day for melting charity.

16.

Take from my mouth the wish of
happy years.

15.

God bless thee, lady.

April

17.

She so lowly, lovely and so loving.

18.

God hath blessed you with a good name.

April

19.

'er shall the sun rise on
such another.

20.

Few words are best. I wish thee luck.

21.

Friend to truth; of soul sincere,
In actions faithful, in honour clear.

A very nice girl you'll find her.

April

22.

You have deserved

High commendation, true applause, and love.

23.

Yet I do fear thy nature,

It is too full o' the milk of human kindness.

April

24.

ou are looked for and called for,
sked for and sought for.

25.

He hath a daily beauty in his life.

26.

heresoever thou mayest tread,
 thy path with flowers spread.

April

27.

Noble in every thought, in every deed
A true friend to the true.

28.

My natural instinct teaches me,
And instinct is important, O!
You're everything you ought to be,
And nothing that you oughtn't, O!

April

29.

God bless thee, lady.

30.

I have heard of the lady, and goodness went with her name.

May

Then let us welcome pleasant spring,
And still the flowery tribute bring,
And still to thee our carol sing,
O, lovely May.

May

1.

In thy face I see
The map of honour,
  truth and loyalty.

2.

She is an earthly paragon.

3.

In life and death alike possessing,
The rich man's love, the poor man's blessin

May

4.

A lucky little lady.

He is as full of valour as of valour.

5.

I cannot hide what I am.

6.

Calm as the river seaward flows,
May thy life be from dawn to close.

May

7.

Born under a propitious star.

Holy, fair and wise is she.

8.

Love all, trust a few,
Do wrong to none.

9.

By thy example teach,
***What few** can practise,*
All can preach.

May

10.

Good fortune guide thee.

He is a marvellous good neighbour.

12.

Her whose worth makes other
    worthies nothing,

She is alone.

11.

A kind heart he hath.

She is a woman, therefore may be woo'd,
She is a woman, therefore may be won.

May

13.

A loving heart and head within.

My man's as true as steel.

14.

Of all say'd yet, mayst thou prove
prospero̶

Of all say'd yet, I wish thee happiness̶

15.

In faith, he is a worthy gentleman,
Exceedingly well-read.

May

16.

Sacred and sweet was all I saw in her.

17.

Fair she is, if that mine eyes be true.

18.

Good fortune guide thee.

May

19.

Sure to charm all is your peculiar fate.

May fortune bless you.

20.

High sparks of honour in thee have I seen

21.

A sage companion and an easy friend.

May

22.

As much good stay with thee
as go with me.

23.

May peace be thy fair guest alway,

Like sunshine gilding each new day.

24.

God save the Queen.

May

25.

Polite, gentle, neat and trim.

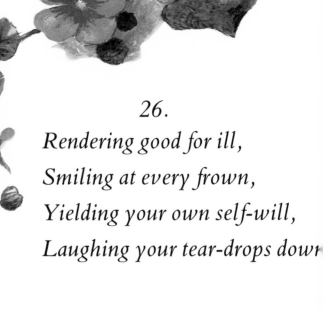

26.

Rendering good for ill,
Smiling at every frown,
Yielding your own self-will,
Laughing your tear-drops down

May

27.
God will prosper thee.

29.
Good fortune guide thee.

28.
How far can I
      praise him?

30.
My man's as true as steel.

May

31.

Among the noblest in the land.

All happiness bechance to thee.

June

1.

Let all the number of the stars give light
To thy fair way.

2.

Fortune and Victory sit on
thy helm

3.

I would applaud thee to the very echo,
That should applaud again.

June

4.

I will believe thou hast a
        mind that suits

With this thy fair and outward
        character.

5.

God bless thee, and put meekness
        in thy mind,

Love, charity, obedience and true duty.

June

6.
*Exceeding wise, fair-spoken
and persuading.*

8.
Your heart's desire be with you

7.
Hourly joys be still upon you.

9.
May fortune bless you.

June

10.

know you have a gentle, noble temper,

soul as even as a calm.

11.

nd she is fair, and fairer than that word

f wondrous virtues.

12.

The rose is red, the violet's blue,

The pink is sweet, and so are you.

June

13.

Faithful, forgiving, full of charity.
He is a marvellous good neighbour.

15.

The God of heaven
Both now and ever bless her.
How far can I praise him?

14.

And those about her,
From her, shall read the perfect ways
of honour.

June

16.
He hath a daily beauty in his life.

18.
She is wise, if I can judge of her.

17.
Full of noble device, of all sorts,
Enchantingly beloved.

19.
The sweetest lady that ever
I looked on.

June

20.

A lucky little lady.

*A proper man, as one shall
see on a summer's day.*

21.

*Her voice was ever soft,
Gentle and low, an excellent thing
in woma*

22.

May fortune bless you.

A sage companion and an easy friend.

June

23.

Still achieving, still pursuing,
Learn to labour and to wait.

Old friends are best.

24.

I dare do all that may become a man,
who dares do more is none.

June

25.

*Large was his bounty,
and his soul sincere.*

26.

*Never idle a moment, but
thrifty and thoughtful of others.*

27.

To bear is to conquer our fate.

June

28.

A maiden fair to see.

29.

The wheel of fortune guide thee.

30.

Ponder well and know the right,
Onward then, and know thy might.
The will to do, the soul to dare.

July

1.

May peace be thy fair guest alway.

2.

Do thy duty; that is best,
Leave unto thy Lord the rest.

July

3.

Be just and fear not.

Old in honours, young in age.

4.

A gracious innocent soul.

5.

Sincere and good.

Half all men's hearts are his.

July

6.

Skilled in every art.

8.

Excellent alike in all.

7.

A graceful dame.

We are born to do benefits.

July

9.

What's brave, what's noble,
Let's do it.

10.

Make use of time,
Let not advantage slip.

11.

Let each man do his best.

July

12.

Good fortune ever find you.

13.

Old Friends are the best.

July

14.

Thou'rt such a touchy, testy, pleasant fellow.

15.

Much joy and favour to you.

July

16.

A full rich nature, free to trust,
Truthful and almost sternly just.

17.

The God of heaven both now and
ever bless thee.

18.

You are looked for and called for,
Asked for and sought for.

19.

True and trusty.

July

20.

hine own wish, wish I thee
in every place.

22.

Holy, pure, and humble of mind,
Blithe of cheer and gentle of mind.

21.

lessings be with them.

July

23.

There never was so wise a man before.

24.

To nobody second
I'm certainly reckoned.

July

25.
Old in honours, young in years.

26.
A cheerful look, a pleasing eye.

27.
He hath an excellent good name.

July

28.

A health to our future,
A sigh for our past,
We love to remember,
We hope to the last.

29.

For truth has such a face and such a mien,
As to be loved needs only to be seen.

The sweetest lady I ever looked on.

July

30.

When you are here, we sigh
with pleasure,

When you are gone, we sigh
with grief.

31.

Let all the number of the stars
give light

To thy fair way.

August

How fair a sight, that nest of gold,
Those wreaths that August's brow enfolds!
Oh, 'tis a goodly sight, and fair,
To see the fields their produce bear.
Waved by the breeze's lingering wing,
So thick, they seem to laugh and sing.

August

1.

*Take from my mouth the
wish of happy years.*

3.

*God in heaven bless thee.
How far can I praise him?*

2.

A very nice girl you'll find her.

4.

Holy, fair and wise is she.

August

5.

My man's as true as steel.

A lucky little lady.

6.

I do love nothing in the world so well as you.

7.

A loyal, just and upright gentleman.

8.

A kind heart he hath.

August

9.

A man he is to all the country dear.

10.

Do thy duty; that is best,
Leave unto thy Lord the rest.

11.

The pink is sweet, and so are you.

12.

Sincere and good.

August

13.

She doeth little kindnesses
Which most leave undone or despise.
Excellent alike in all.

14.

The hand that made you fair
Hath made you good.

15.

A kind heart he hath.

August

16.

Much joy and favour to you.

A damsel fair to see.

17.

Steady of heart and stout of hand.
Your heart's desire be with you.

August

18.

The very heart of kindness.

20.

Busy after others good,
For herself the last to care.

19.

She so lowly, lovely and so loving.

August

21.

What do you think of me?
As of a man faithful and honourable.

22.

Of many good I think him bes

August

24.

A voice of comfort, an open hand of help – A splendid person.

25.

The very heart of kindness.

Do thy duty; that is best,
Leave unto thy Lord the rest.

23.

Long may you live in fortune.

August

26.

*There never was so wise
a man before.*

28.

True she is.

27.

The sweetest lady I ever looked on.

August

29.

We are born to do benefits.

30.

Half all men's hearts are his.

31.

Rendering good for ill,
Smiling at every frown.
Yielding your own self-will,
Laughing your tear-drops down.

September.

Harvests were gathered in; and wild with
the winds of September
Wrestled the trees of the forest, as
Jacob of old with the angel . . .
Filled was the air with a dreamy and
magical light; and the landscape
Lay as if new created in all the
freshness of childhood.

September

1.

True to your word, your work, and your friend.

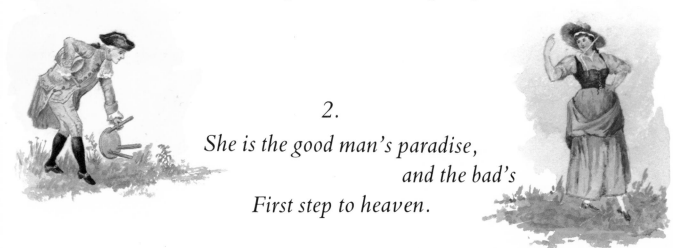

2.

She is the good man's paradise,
and the bad's
First step to heaven.

September

3.

he is noblest, being good.

y, every inch a king.

5.

A thing of beauty is a joy for ever.

4.

A cold and clear-cut face

Perfectly beautiful.

6.

In thy face I see

The map of honour, truth
and loyalty.

September

7.

A full rich nature, free to trust,
Truthful and almost sternly just.
The very heart of kindness.

9.

Excellent alike in all.

8.

Glad greeting to you friend this day,
Good fortune ever find you.

September

10.

Holy, pure, and humble of mind,
Blithe of cheer and gentle of mind.

12.

She is lovely, constant, kind.

11.

In the right place is his heart.

September

13.

Whate'er he did was done with so much ease,
In him alone, 'twas natural to please.

14.

Oh, what a noble character is this!

September

15.

A true friend to the true.

16.

Love all, trust a few,
Do wrong to none.

17.

Make use of time,
Let not advantage slip.

September

18.

A damsel fair to see.

19.

True and trusty.

20.

She is constant, lovely, kind.

September

21.

rained for either camp or court,
kilful in each manly sport.

22.

And honours without end
hall surround thee on every side,
And attend thee night and day.

23.

There never was so wise a man
before.

24.

Let us then be up and doing,
With a heart for every fate.
Still achieving, still pursuing,
Learn to labour and to wait.

September

25.

She is noblest, being good.

27.

*'Tis the greatest folly
Not to be jolly,
That's what I think.*

26.

*Calm as the river seaward flows,
May thy life be from dawn to close.*

September

28.

Courteous by nature, not by rule,
Warm-hearted, and of cordial face.

30.

How far can I praise him?

29.

Can greet a friend and grasp a foe,
Can take a jest, and give a blow.
The very heart of kindness.

OCTOBER.

When Summer goes then shadows creep
Across the world of trees and flowers;
The birds a solemn silence keep
Through Autumn's slowly darkening hours.

October

1.

*Not enjoyment and not sorrow
Is our destined end or way.
But to act that each tomorrow
Finds us farther than today.*

2.

*Fair on earth shall be thy fame
As thy face is fair.*

3.

*A man of forecast and of thrift,
And of a shrewd and careful mind.*

October

4.

Oh, what a noble character is this!
Be as they presence is,
Gracious and kind.

5.

Thou art strong and great, a hero.

6.

To nobody second
I'm certainly reckoned.

October

7.

Fair and prosperous be thy life.

8.

A day for toil, an hour for sport,
But for a friend is life too short.

9.

Long may you live in fortune.

October

10.

One of those who wins our hearts
By show of sympathy.

11.

A very nice girl you'll find her.

October

12.

Glad greeting to you friend this day,
Good fortune ever find you.

13.

For contemplation he, and valour form'd,
For softness she, and sweet attractive grace.

October

14.

Serenely moving on her way
In hours of trial and dismay.

15.

A loyal, just and
            upright gentleman.

16.

For truth hath such a face and such a mien,
As to be loved needs only to be seen.

October

17.
A full rich nature, free to trust,
Truthful and almost sternly just.

18.
The gentleman is full of virtue,
bounty, worth and qualities.

October

19.

And may all holy angels guard thee.

20.

If all my wishes could prevail
To make existence fair,
Then all the world should envy thee,
Exempt from every care.

October

23.

Skilled in every art.

21.

The very heart of kindness.

22.

Holy, pure, and humble of mind,
Blithe of cheer and gentle of mind.

October

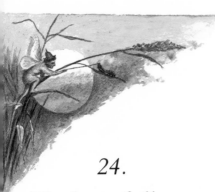

24.

The best of all,
Blest with plain reason and sober sense.

25.

The roughest road often leads
to the smoothest fortune.

26.

The best of all,
Amongst the rarest of good ones.

27.

Be as thy presence is,
Gracious and kind.

October

28.

A man more pure, and bold and just,
Was never born into the world.

29.

Gallant, graceful, gentle, tall,
Fairest, noblest, best of all.

October

30.

His better does not breathe upon the earth.

31.

He hath a daily beauty in his life.

God bless thee, lady.

NOVEMBER.

Days are drear
and skies are overcast,
But love will warm
our hearts
Whate'er betide.

November

2.

*Fair on earth shall be
thy fame*

As thy face is fair.

1.

Though I am no judge of such matters,
I'm sure he's a talented man.

November

3.

A man not of words but of actions.

5.

Excellent alike in all.

4.

We have found you great and noble.

November

6.

He is a marvellous good neighbour.

8.

True she is.

7.

She is lovely, constant, kind.

9.

I wish you all the joy that you can wish.

November

10.

When you are here, we sigh with pleasure,
When you are gone, we sigh with grief.

11.

She doeth little kindnesses
Which most leave undone or despise.

November

12.

The very pattern girl of girls.

13.

The rose is red, the violet's blue,
The pink is sweet, and so are you

14.

Not enjoyment and not sorrow
Is our destined end or way.
But to act that each tomorrow
Finds us farther than today.

November

15.

Serenely moving on her way
In hours of trial and dismay.

17.

May fortune bless you.

16.

A true friend to the true.

November

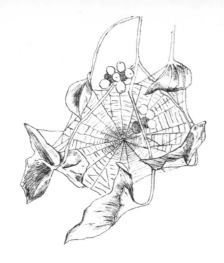

18.

And honours without end
Shall surround thee on every side
And attend thee night and day.

19.

Books were his passion and delight.

20.

Wheresoever thou mayst tread,
Be thy path with flowers spread.

November

21.

say
ust what I think, and nothing
iore or less,
And when I pray, my heart is
i my prayer.
cannot say one thing and mean
nother.

22.

Serene, and resolute and still,
And calm and self-possessed.

November

23.

She's so sweet, you see,
She's the girl for me.

24.

For he is fair to look upon, and comely.

25.

She is noblest, being good.

November

26.

A full rich nature, free to trust,

Truthful and almost sternly just.

27.

The very pattern girl of girls.

Thou art strong and great, a hero.

November

28.

*I wish you all the joy that
you can wish.*

30.

*Of very reverend reputation,
Of credit infinite, highly belove*

29.

*My natural instinct teaches me,
And instinct is important, O!
You're everything you ought to be,
and nothing that you ought'nt, O!*

Goodbye to old sorrow, grief, and unrest!
Bury them deep in the Old Year's breast;
And welcome the joy that lies apart,
Waiting for us in the New Year's heart.

December

1.

True she is.

3.

We are born to do benefit.

2.

God be with you now and ever,
God protect and be your stay.

4.

Skilled in every art.

December

5.

A voice of comfort, an open hand of help. A splendid person.

6.

A graceful dame.

7.

For every virtue, every work renowned,
Sincere, plain-hearted, hospitable, kind.

December

8.

Good fortune ever find you.

10.

Sweets to the sweet.

9.

Be to yourself
As you would to your
friend.

11.

God be with you all.

December

12.

May peace be thy fair guest alway,
Like sunshine gilding each new day.

13.

To those that know thee, no words can paint,
To those who know thee, all words are faint.

December

14.

True friendship between man,
And man is infinite and immortal.

15.

Half all men's hearts are his.

16.

If all my wishes could prevail
To make existence fair,
Then all the world should envy thee,
Exempt from every care.

December

17.

Be as thy presence is,
Gracious and kind.

18.

Hope with eyes of sunny seed,
Smile thee on to power and deed.

19.

Love all, trust a few,
Do wrong to none.

December

20.

Do thy duty; that is best,
Leave unto thy Lord the rest.

21.

Serenely moving on her way
In hours of trial and dismay.

December

22.

You are looked for and
called for, and asked for
and sought for.

23.

Let us then be up and doing,
With a heart for every fate.
Still achieving, still pursuing,
Learn to labour and to wait.

December

24.

He hath an excellent good name.

25.

We speak of a Merry Christmas,
And many a Happy New Year.

26.

In all things
Mindful not of herself, but
bearing the burden of others.

December

27.

The dearest friend to me, the kindest man.
The best conditioned and unwearied spirit,
In doing courtesies.

28.

Serene, and resolute and still,
And calm and self-possessed.

December

29.

Beautiful in form and feature,
Lovely as the day,
Can there be so fair a creature,
Formed of common clay?

30.

For he was great of heart, magnanimous,
Courtly, courageous.

December

31.

Never idle a moment, but thrifty and thoughtful of others.

Old year, you must not go;
So long as you have been with us,
Such joy as you have seen with us,
Old year, you shall not go.

Old year, you shall not die;
We did so laugh and cry with you,
I've half a mind to die with you,
Old year, if you must die.